E
Evincepub
Publishing

Evincepub Publishing

Parijat Extension, Bilaspur, Chhattisgarh 495001
First Published by Evincepub Publishing 2020
Copyright © Dr.Satyanarayan Mishra 2020
All Rights Reserved.
ISBN: 978-93-90197-05-7

TIME

WILL

TWIST

A collection of poems

Dr. Satyanarayan Mishra

About The Book

This is the sixth English poetry book of the poet. There are thirty two poems of various types in this presentation. The title of the book "Time will twist "is based on one of the poems of the book. The poems have their typical poetic composition each carrying some short of messages useful for the society. The poems are simple, meaningful and well-structured having contents that will undoubtedly be appreciated by readers. Evincepub Publishing has done a great job in publishing the contents in the form of a book.

CONTENTS

WORDS TALK

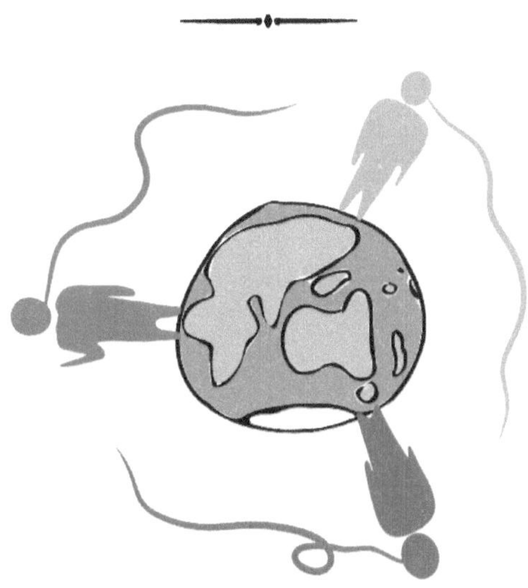

Words also appear romantic
Yes of course.
Most of the times
The words lose their temper.
May be pleasant for others
The words play a messy game,
Turbulent minds get trapped.
This time too,
They came from your lips with love wrapped
I got bewildered,
by those soothing ' hey' and 'hello'
Forgot my feelings.
This time too the words played
the naughty game,

Could not make out their dealings
This time the foggy weather,
chilly winter collapsed,
Said, at last, a 'bye'
Spring's cuckoo now yet to sing,
either love of truth or lie.

O LORD

O Lord, O Lord, where do you prefer to stay
in the cave of great Hills or idols of clay?
Do you like to rest in the piece of hard stone
or else reside in the devotees' sweet tone?
Ever do you occupy place inside the holy shrine
Temple gate do you like where people make a
line?
In the river, in the moon, hill or shore, where?
where nature plays the game, do you stay there?
Do you stay in the slum or sky, do you like poor
Do you love a beggar, labourer or
Wealthy man's offer?
Do you only allow men or women, either of any
genders
Are you a rock hard spirit or a God of heart
tender?

Do you like struggle or conflict, logic, argument
ever
Do you accept, the fact that the man is more
clever?
Who are you, where are you may please give
some notion
they say that they never see you, but you make
the earth's motion.

TODAY AND TOMORROW

The Sun arrives as usual
As any other day
However, appears lazy
As if taking rest and emerging
Hesitantly from the east abode
It greets, greets with some hope
Some charming moments
Pleasurable plans and gossip
jolly get-together moments
Why it is so, unlike any other
Stress prone moments,
Challenges, tasks and hangover
On the reply, the Sun smiles,
looking bit relaxed
Hello... Says the Sun
It's my day
a long-cherished, Sunday.

O Sunday --we ever wait only
to meet you once in seven days.
I can't understand
It's not that much pleasurable
Looking towards the heap of
dirty clothes, list of domestic exigencies and
demands
Dear Sun, will you please grant
Two of your such days
In a week, the Sun does not respond
It looks towards the west
The horizon is still some distance away
Hurriedly it skips without
the response, the setting too
So attractive,
I sigh.. I have to wait and plan for tomorrow.
Tomorrow is not the Stars' day, the Sunday.
It belongs to the Moon.

MOOD

The morning sky was clear
Blue background suddenly turned Grey
Somewhere blackish too
White patches concentrated
The background turned cloudy
The sky too looked moody
It often turns moody
independent of our wish
The mood of the sky brings a twinkle
of stars, the mesmerizing moon rays and
the dazzling Sun too.
The mood of sky captures rainbows
vibrates with thunder,
spark of lightning sometimes
Zigzag flashes cut the backdrop brilliantly
The mood of heaven gets tuned,
assimilates with the mood of earth.
Earth calls the sky, to approach
with a heavenly watery kiss.

The downpour drips
Morning earth gets drenched
My mood also changes
It is going to be a rainy day
The childhood memory
gets ignited,
Drench in drops
Get wet, dance and enjoy
Alas, impossible now
The body will not manage
The mood and body mismatch
I grumble on earth and sky
Why my mood and body mismatch
whereas in case of them.
That's not a problem.

EYES

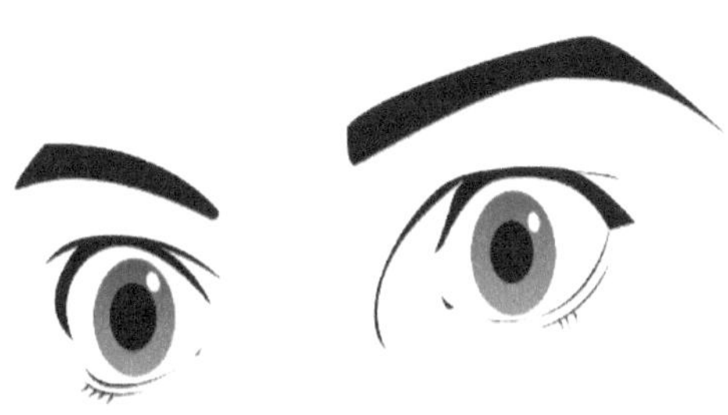

Those were too dark
Sometimes look furious
often vigilant like a CCTV cam
I retreat, sometimes
anticipating the strike in a subtle form
That dark circles whirl all around
Start looking from the Galaxy to Earth
Gazing curiously or mercilessly.
those eyes do not melt easily
like the tearful eyes
Sometimes eyes too respond
to the needy, to a heart of noble soul while
calling helplessly
Nowadays the eyes look callous
not even responding to the undressing, crime, or
unlawful
dealings even at their throne.

In their place of the shrine
It's the black circles, in anguish
or indifference, in love or teaching
the lesson, in rewarding or throwing away
None can tell, how, when, where the black
circular eyes will seize one red-handed.

PUBLIC FIGURE

Where are you, my Lord?
Come and appear
I need your help
You are the Lord, you are the God
The silence prevails
The followers' roar resonates
The anticipation and hope
engulf the mind
Hours after hours
Sound of conch, drum and bell
resounds in the atmosphere
The Baba shouts and shouts
O God, Please appear, Please show us your face
An intelligent disciple murmurs
What a fool... Why do I come here?
Ever the Lord takes a form!

The side devotee with tearful eyes
embraces him, what you say, friend?
The Guru has seen HIM earlier
that's why he calls
but the question is not what
you asked.
The question is
Does God appear in Public?
The naughty follower tells
may be this time, Do you know our
Guruji's profile? He is a Public Figure.

NIGHT

Why the nights are dark?
to suit for rest or relax
or to look at the sky and star
who had a little spark
or it is for the nocturnal
beings to a quest for the hunt
or to go on a mission
for those who can't come to the front.
Night is dark
as dark as coal
It's no better than a tunnel
Where hides the face of
dormant soul.
It's a night to celebrate for the Moon

for the river and the sea
for the dream
and sweet company of my dear
Else what can be the plea?

THERE MAY BE SOME CHANGE

Suddenly the sky was turning grey
slowly the patches of smoky clouds
Expanded extending its exterior
It looks furious
Perhaps a storm may happen
Droplets trickle
from the roof above
The drops too condense in mass
may be the pouring bullets or bulbs
bombard with a typical cracking noise...
The rain may be of ice drops
rarely *nature* manipulates
the form of liquid to solid
It might be a stone rain, ice rain
A rain of pleasure which still captures
the childhood mind
A rain of displeasure for that poor fellow

Whose roof is likely to be damaged
why are you scared? Uncle
In reply the old man tried to speak something
some short hardly audible voice
hit my ear...Fani
I said yes... *Nature* is funny
The old man asked curiosity
to understand what I told
or expecting some exchange of help from me...
I just told... in his understandable language
"Do not be scared
Every storm is not Fani
Wait and see.
There may be some change"
The man looked nervous
looked again towards his small cottage,
towards me, again towards the sky
He smiled...and told.
See dear... The clouds are clearing.
The sky is now getting cleaner wiping its all
dusty patches of prints,
This is high time to celebrate...
Nature plays fun...
And all plays are not disastrous.

WHAT WORSE CAN HAPPEN

Star is falling
Look, look the star is falling
yelled the boy
It's no unusual, said the friend
I have seen it many times.
Did anything happen to you?
Why and what...queried the friend
The first boy told
It is a bad omen
predecessors told

Don't believe, assured the friend
See again
another is falling

With a jet speed going to strike the surface.
what a view like the game of a firecracker
The boy took his cell
captured the falling star
The meteor was imprisoned at last
He will share it,
show it
A phenomenon to be viewed
Erase it...
threatened the friend
Why are you not happy
When others will see
and like me?.. asked the boy.
No... nothing like that...said the friend
we believe it is not a good scenery.
But you told, nothing happened to you
"I had seen it, not shared
Open and see first
What you have captured "said the second.
The first boy opened the gallery
an elongated band of white light
Moving downwards was there
See now, this is there
The second boy got fascinated
Please share this with me
The boy assured, he will do
later the boy returned home
with his cell
He was anxious.

What worse can happen to him!
"Probably the angry father
Who was threatening till date
may snatch the device from him"....
Meteor effect at worst bring this
May it not happen
The boy murmured the prayer in silence
In favour of the stars, planets and heaven.

BLOOD AND PET

I kept it for many days
as if it is my child
took all care ...nourishing,
feeding, cleaning and loving
it was my kid as if
it never betrayed me
always kept my gate secured

'no disturbance please...'
the barking itself endowed with
the message
forget tress passers
even if a bird
a snake
an insect intruder
it will examine with introspecting eyes
until it grew to a big hound

I decided to dispose
but it was not mentally prepared
it returned after some days
again from my friend's house
no..no
you stay with me
the old man assured
else I will feel lonely
my son has mailed
he will not return to me
he thanks what I did
but simultaneously tried to convince
It is every father's duty also.
He quotes great seer
"Expectation causes pain and misery"
Let me reconcile, my pet
Let me live without my blood
but not without my pet.

MAKE IT FREE

When everything is over
come and bow your head down
Else you need not knock
the door, no need to frown
Very nature of human being
He forgets after he gets
he wants always some instant reply,
Never has he waited
Having strength in hand and foot,
man desperately stares at the statue
the god too seems callous knowingly
reviewing the vice and virtue
Doing anything irrespective of moral
The man praise God for only excuses
The very nature of human
being always of course amuses

Now the crisis, cure in your hand
what the temple and God will do
At least keep the shrine clean and safety
make it free from flue
Hands your earn vice and virtue
hands give you the outcome
handless deity silently suggests
'maintain hygiene norm'.

(Note-the poem is composed at the time of the spread of Covid 19)

TIME WILL TWIST

:
When nature
wants to create
there are numerous
new forms
none can obstruct, none can decline
these are natural norms
Nature knows you better ever
than others else know
since you are ever Nature's product
she knows every key of your grow
She knows your strength
knows your mind
and the weakness of your too
not easy always to maintain the pace or halt
never always there is a clue

It may be a human brain, the human mind
that can create an evil
it may be more ghastly
when very nature forms the devil
Nature mutates, nature forms
nature is too humorous
nature smiles seeing the
plight, what a ghastly virus
The invincible kind should now mind
how should be the style and the life!
Time will twist testing the
patience ' halt' or 'face the knife'
Time has tested human strength
new things will come
the life will again rotate
but for the moment
it is the viral term.

(Note-the poem is composed at the time of the spread of Covid 19)

NO ODD IN IT

The colors stuck to the palms
fingers cheeks and face
Was unable to wash those away
So sticky was the trace

Washed then and then
rubbed the patches with eager
all attempt was in vein
so intense was the vigour

Added many more lotion
having a notion it may dilute the patches
none should laugh at me
seeing the color mismatches

Nothing could dilute the effect
as if glued to my skin
As if the Holi color decided
not to leave a day after even

The stains were looking now
as if they are faded but alive
The Holi memory will not vanish soon
Saying that it will thrive

It will keep the memory of love and tie
Want to stay some more
Decided to leave those color as it was
no odd in it further.

COLOR GAME

Life sometimes looks
Colorless, deprived of glamour, fanciful moments
Exhausted...
Asking myself
The answer was not there...
Why and how
who looted the rhythm
who destroyed the glee
who catastrophically attacked
on the hues of my existence?
Looking towards the sky
sometimes, the vast blueness
Seems to be the culprit
in taking away my color
No ...no... The sky reluctantly
replied... am vast, colorful
from time immemorial

who cares for yours
The same reply came from the blue sea...
The rainbow spectrum...
Did not even admit if they would have
taken away my hues
The greenish grass patches
The Grey deserted land
The white hilly ice heaps
The color patched caterpillar
Each on asking refused to
Being enriched with my color
Then who looted it
I screamed... Who...Who?
The echo reverberated
The morning appeared with a handful of colors,
The sky, the sea, the dunes,
the creatures all along shouted,
clapped all together.
Take your color back...
Celebrate, all colors are gifted to you again
I woke up... Greeted all
Their Color will not diminish
By gifting to me and thousands of like me
Why they will take my color
A shy soul within me thanked those with
heartfelt
Gratefulness
My inner voice told
Celebrate, celebrate whatever the remaining

color you have
Now *Nature* is with you
Who can steal your pleasure.?

SOLE SAVIOUR

Dream... O my dear,
Sweat storehouse of my fantasy
Where you hide in daylight?
appear in dreaded or nice costumes of fancy
Sometimes I seek your gracious
presence in the day of light
When everything robbed of from me
I too never find you easily,
except for certain hours of the night
Carrying my stubborn thoughts
Which could neither be filled up nor vanished
You, my favorite guest,
appear in a lovely gesture
keeping my eyelids tight
You promise me a lot, assure me

with healthy offers of tomorrow
I breathe easy for a moment
Forgetting the real moments of sorrow
plenty of wealth and
Myriads of colorful presents
A lovely bride and flowering garden
....all look in that hours decent
Alas.. I miss you a lot nowadays
with increasing agonizing barrier
Nights are too limited for me as days
O Goddess of the dream
You are my sole saviour.

WOMAN OF GRACE

Who showed you
The stable field of this earth
From the uncertainty of ethereal frame
Who gave you this rare birth
Who brought you from the womb
Of darkness and limited movement
Showing you the path of light
To grow, act and engagement
From whom you got the life
Got the body of flesh and bone
Who made you welcome
The planet with a baby crying tone
Who made you to groom and bloom
To a perfect man of the time
Who fed you since your birth

Who touched you with love sublime
Who loved you more than the self?
Helped to be a lover of youth
Turned you to a perfect human
Shredding everything for your growth
Know that you are more stable
Invincible, stubborn in race
The lady, who framed you in shape.

DAUGHTER OF POETESS

O mother, Poetess Mother
Everything you did for me
I saw the land and light
found the river and tree
Saw the people, tasted the love
None is better than you
Copied the very act of doing
Wearing, adjusting with new
Learnt the lesson of worship
followed the ways you taught
O mother, my lovely mother
Nothing to condemn my lot
What I did it's your action
They say you are in me
I am the mother in disguise
In my cute girl body be

Am the incarnated being too
I repeat the deeds of your
How much I do and not do
can't duplicate, am sure
I have the same virtues whatever
You had with you
They say, not I, my mom
What is with me new
Only thing is, I can say
I can't copy your mind
Neither your writings of poems
I can create,
you were a special kind
You are my poetess mother
you are unique and your poems too
Your life could write and recite
I was unborn then, what could I do.

MORE TOUCH PLEASE LEND

O tear, O tear, you are my dear
When nobody is there only you see and hear
When none has time to listen
You respond to the pain
When none is giving the company
You all along the cheeks drain
Drops of pearl like Tears flow
Wetting the eye and my look
None can write or read my agony
Only you write my book
Nobody can paint my pain
You only give it a sense
In the absence of your company
My pain will be multiplied and dense
You flow in pleasure, drip in pain

You are my sensible friend
Please do not leave me along the way of life
More touch... Please lend.

THREE 'P'

Poem

Not a beautiful literary piece
whatever you can fix
maybe somehow some sweet topic
but how it is useful to the public.

Poet

A genius or innovative creator
No doubt an expert word player
His letters and words so inspiring
Always a source of life with honest aspiring
Unless mind and heart free from ego
none remembers the charismatic
brand and logo.

Pen

Auspicious always with a mystic flow
creator always with words and lines in a row
Captures the sudden flashes may even or odd
Irrespective of time
Interprets the unique intuitive code.

WHERE

Where are those
future tellers
who can well advance
guide
where are those gurus
and babas who can
save from hazardous tide?

May our faith in supreme power
guide and give us strength
it should not be a false belief
founded on blind faith.

Our inner spirit guides us
gives strength to face days
it is our confidence and trust
which will bring new rays.

SEASON SPEAKS

The breeze thrills
the wind intoxicates the psyche
a season of blooming
budding, bewitching and tempting
simultaneously a hidden
toxic warning
seasonal prompting at the backdrop
take care of pollens
particles and toxins

Nature always gives a warning signal
Creation is always endowed with
a threat of annihilation.

TRUE BEAUTY

Originally the evening
and nights
are silent and dark
Adding color and brightness
by light and sound
chaos and commotion
they seem to alter
but again return to original get up
when there is an opportunity
the true beauty of nature lies in naturalness.

LOCK, LIVE AND LOVE

Sometimes
It is imposed, in whatever way
Whatever it may, accept or not,
By divine *nature*
To control the race, bring down
the life's pace and uneven hasty gesture.

None can convince, none can train, none can
make him learn
except for the fear of danger, threat
Suffering and loss of some kind.
The man is becoming most restless, most
unstable
forgetting the rest of the body
an uneven race has snatched
the quietness, creating the

huge malady.
Some halt he needs some break
Too in life, unless
haunted by the time
forgetting the need for rest
and relax, supposes
other as prime.
Lock, live and love the leisure
be it any way
Likely to get it even by force
none can divert you else, distract from race
except for compulsion from your course.
Need makes one perfect and innovative
Compulsion brings ways
Above all, he is human no doubt
He is otherwise crazed.

Dr. Satyanarayan Mishra

POETRY WILL REMAIN EVER

Poetry, O Poetry
shine in the realm of literature
Ever having your history
you are sublime, you are eternal
you are the art of the age
be romantic or sadistic
as the primordial hymn of the sage
You are the song, too the emotion
captured ever in ecstasy
You are the verse, also the version
also a dreamer's fantasy
Wordsworth, Eliot, Spenser
or Milton be Sylvia or Brown
Remembered today for their
pen, from a remote village to town
Spontaneous you stream always

Poet's heart is a source
Poet's mind too is so drenched
in poetry ..It is the destination of course
People will go, the poet will go,
but poetry will remain ever
Drenching the passionate readers 'mind
with the special flavor.

FEW LINES

Curb your action curtail the plan
wait for few days
Come and co-operate, high time now
no need of any praise
Obvious it is a painful time like
home lock
Otherwise is no option there
else to avoid the flock
Read the guideline obey them too
robust you might be
Regular cleansing do and teach
real remedy key
Odd days no doubt, O dear all
malady will be faced
Only the human may sustain it,

as experience-based
Never you take unwanted risk
no need to be hasty
None will suffer the pain for other
may it bitter or tasty
Alas, the days should be normal
again restore the pace
Act consciously without hesitation
anticipate days fresh.

SHRED THE CURTAIN

Accumulating too
much wealth
where will it be there
after you quit this earth
Gathering too much
land and money
where will you land then
Is this the aim of your very birth?
a cluster of prizes, money
and memento
May decorate your cupboard now
who sees who will preserve those
or not, why ,where and how

Praises and praisers will
Not be then when you no longer in the limelight
What's the meaning of your too
Many men gathering none will
For your cause fight
Running after false prestige
and earning, being trapped under prejudice
How worthy it appears to you
These are no way better than foolish

Money made man, money made publicity
may dazzle for an instant
Unless one owns persistency of talent
Everything will be at distant
Aware, be active, earn for livelihood
Acquire the knowledge instead
Shred the curtain of falsehood and vanity
Leave those having vested.

MOTIVATION

Motivation
The only way to marching
towards destination

Motivation
Without which
Survival will be not possible,
life will be only a burden.

Inspiration
unique way
to creative action
Inspiration
Comes from the core
dazzling the spirit of innovation.

THREE HOPES

Sleep

You should not
be partial
you should not
be waiting for the invitation
you should naturally arrive and depart
when mind and body need.

Dream

Please avoid hitting me in day
wait please till am trapped in deep hypnosis
of sleep
You are healer, you are my subconscious
projector

For a moment let me be gifted
with all the fulfillments
irrespective of hard reality.

Nightmare

Please leave me this time
I need a sound sleep
a good dream
other than that
no intruder of painful flashback
please leave me at least.

A PSYCHE BETRAYED

Ventilating
Since am trapped
In a human body
Is it not a plan for suffering
By taking my parents away to heaven
Before I quit this world
A psyche betrayed.
Is it not a conspiracy
To push me to this ocean of life and death
Where I don't know swimming
Is it not a conspiracy to see me struggle
For bread and butter till I quit
Is it not...Is it not
To tell me to compete

To fight
With the same beings who are my own
Is it not making a joke and see
How I succeed or fail
Is it not a conspiracy to give duality of mortality
with consciousness and thought
Never-ending desire
for immortality
so again
who can tell
pushed to a circumstance of odds
the eventuality of death and drowning
A conspiracy of nature or man
Of technology or intelligence.

LET US PLAY

Oh! Puppy, O my Kitty
Hey my little doll
Come and let us play
I am free for all
Don't shout or sound much
Mommy may feel angry
My papa is outside
Serving the people hungry
I will give you food and care
All you need here
Let us play an indoor game
With fun and cheer.

BODY LANGUAGE

What the sparrow was chirping
Perhaps it was searching for grains
I really enjoyed seeing
As the chameleon was majestically staring from
the branch of a nearby plant
Gesturing the head times to time ....
Couldn't comprehend for what reason, does it
nod and gesture?
The household dog was barking
From the chains
I understand, might be for food or companion
Numerous pets and creepy crawlies
have their dialects
The man in torn dress and appearance
Showed up on the entryway.

He was hard of hearing or stupid
He was demonstrating some gestures
May be in need of cash
Or nourishment or dress
Asked..What?
He laughed...went away
Maybe could not get me
Returned after some time
Asked for a blossom from my nursery
The single bloom
I gave over
He giggled like a mad
Took a gander at me with cherishing eyes left
He murmured
I need love ...a love-filled heart.

SORE

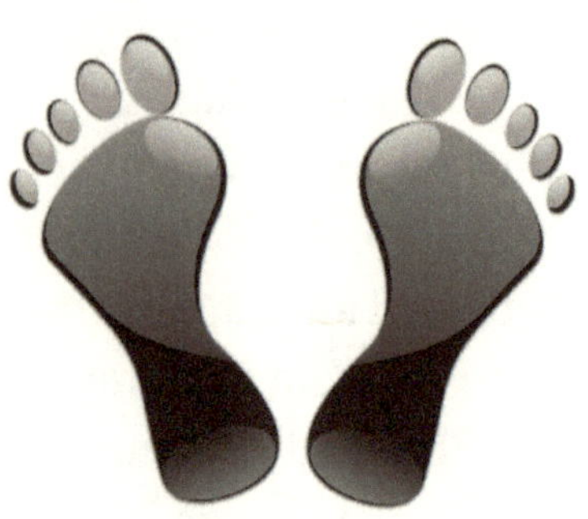

Yes, footsore is there
But we don't care
Our life is not well-defined
You may call us unrefined
Sore in our mind too
But the body can sustain the Loo
Our way is infinite
Time has made us tight
Sore in our foot indeed
Look at our elder and kid
Sore in our stomach ever
But we need no favor.